The Night the Stars Went Out

SUZ HUGHES

PICTURE WINDOW BOOKS
a capstone imprint

For Margaret and Tony

The Night the Stars Went Out is published by
Picture Window Books, a Capstone imprint
1710 Roe Crest Drive
North Mankato, Minnesota 56003
www.mycapstone.com

Library of Congress Cataloging-in-Publication Data is available on
the Library of Congress website.

ISBN 978-1-62370-745-3 (paper over board)
ISBN 978-1-5158-0214-3 (library binding)
ISBN 978-1-78202-516-0 (eBook PDF)

Summary: Alien was the star controller for the entire galaxy, which was
a big job for a very little alien. One night something disastrous happens,
and Alien faces the biggest problem of his life. Will Alien be able to
fix the stars? With a focus on friendship and problem solving, this
picture book is a treat for everyone.

Designer: Lori Bye

Printed and bound in China.
032016   009597F16

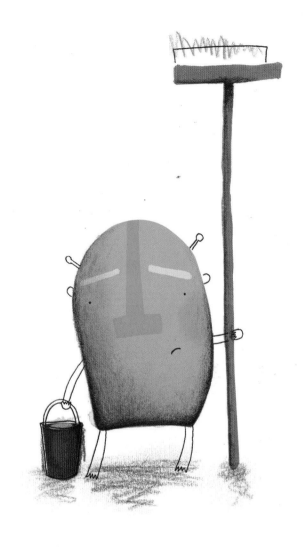

There once was a tiny alien with a very BIG job.

Alien was a star shiner. Every night, he kept the stars shining. Alien took his job VERY seriously — maybe a bit too seriously.

Alien never took time off to do anything fun, and he didn't have any friends.

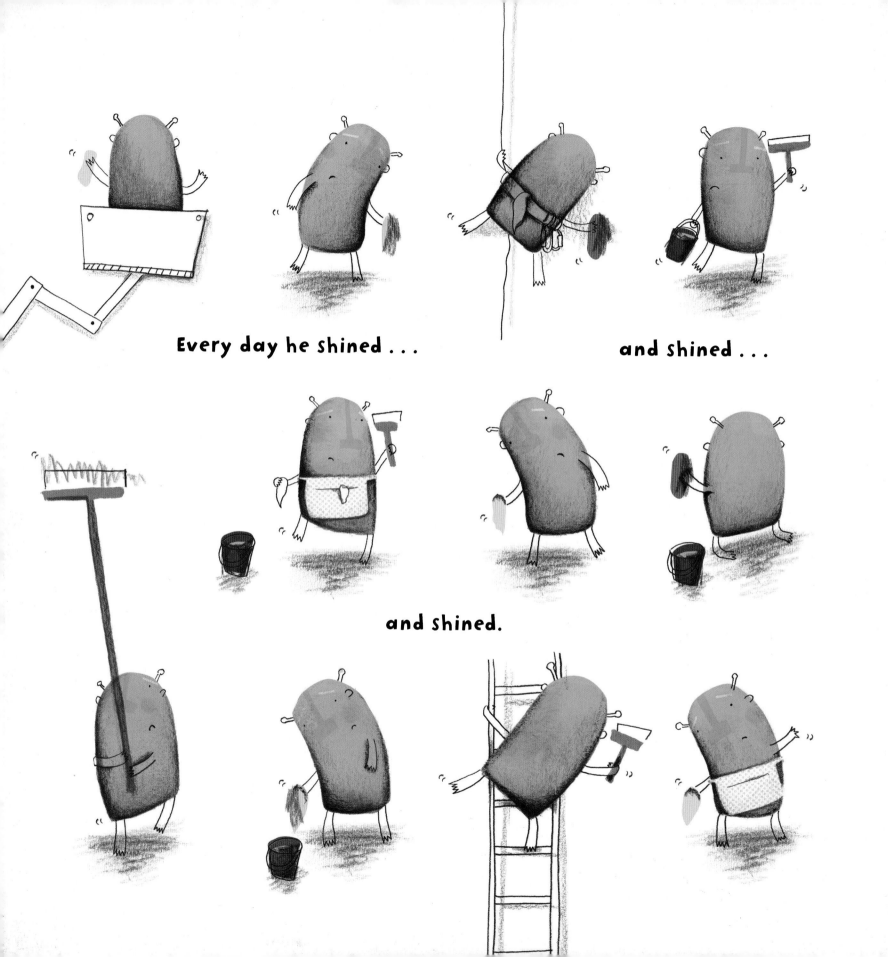

Every day he shined . . .

and shined . . .

and shined.

Shining is all he did! But one night,
something disastrous happened . . .

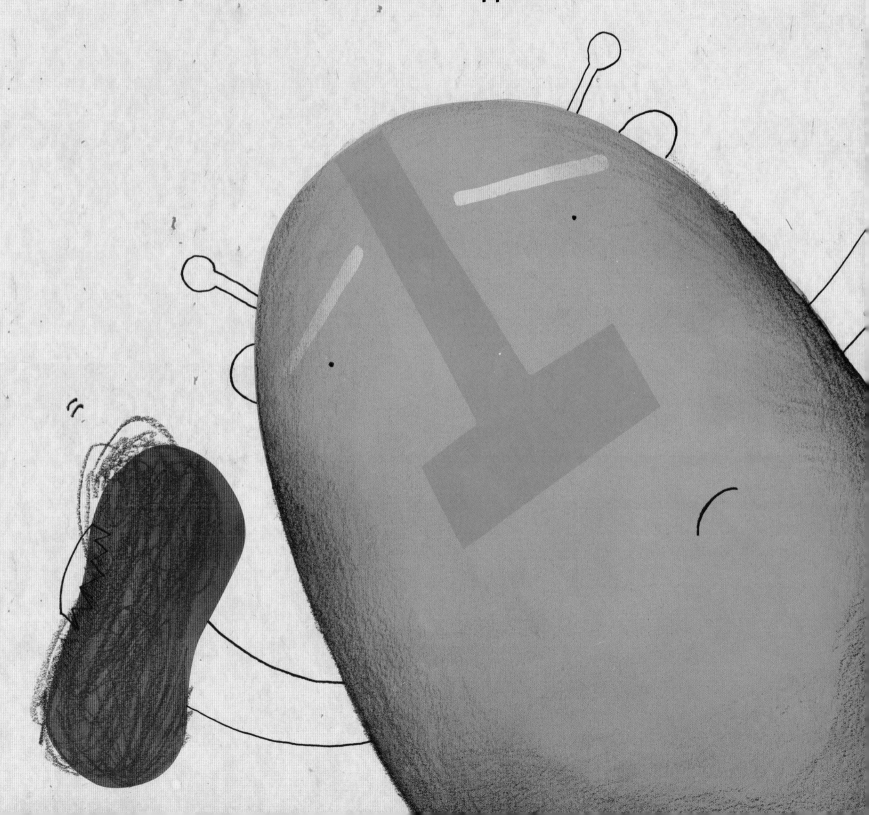

The stars went out!

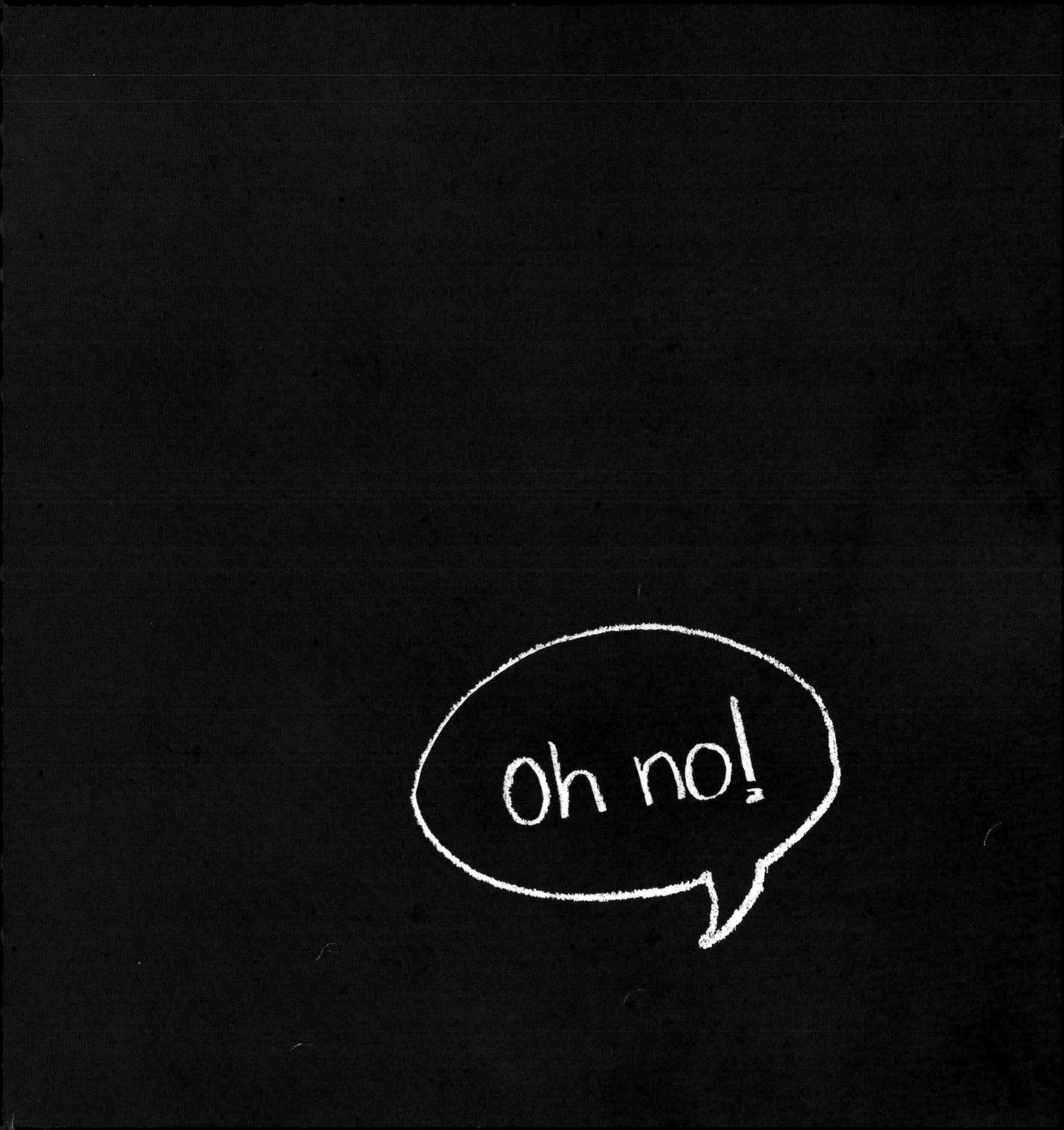
Oh no!

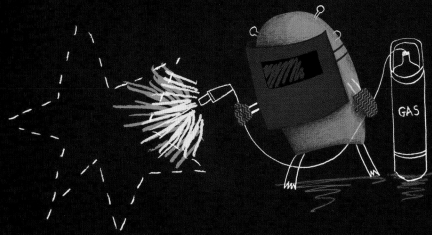

"Did I shine the stars too much?" Alien wondered.

He tried everything to fix the problem, but nothing worked.

Alien was desperate, so he called the Star Helpline.
They told him he needed a magic varnish, but the
varnish was only sold on a faraway planet called Earth.

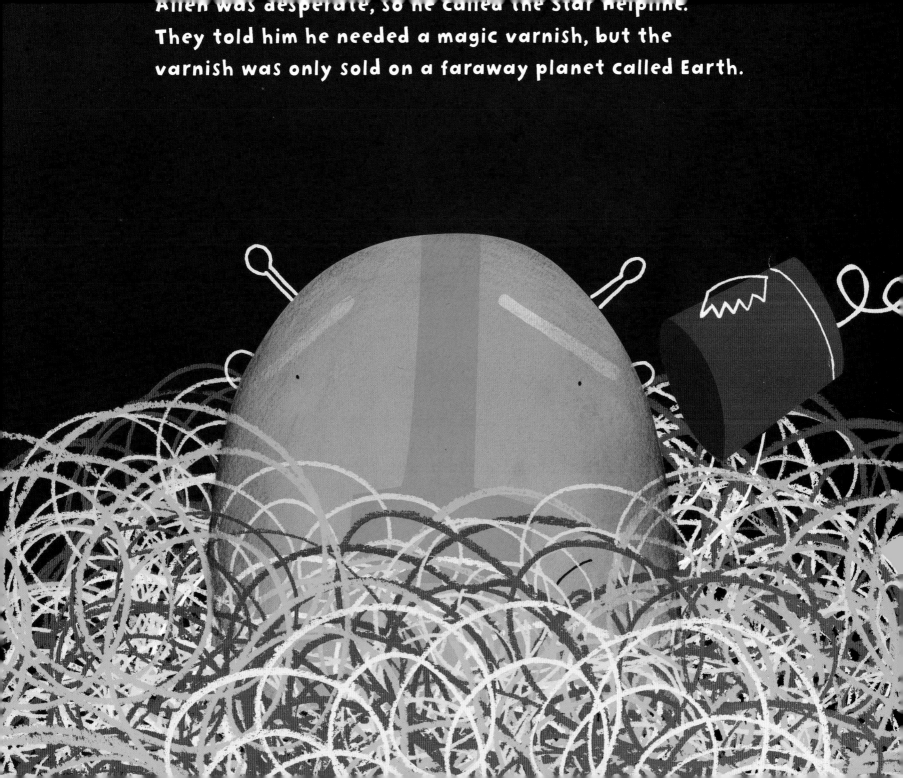

Alien changed into his best human disguise and set off right away. It was a long trip.

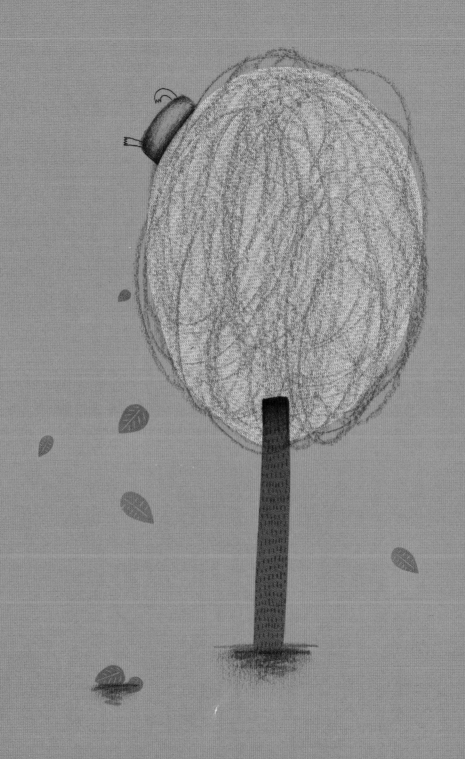

Alien hadn't planned for this, and he got himself into a bit of a tangle.

Alien kept yelling and finally got the attention of a young boy and his dog.

"Hello. Can you help me, please?" Alien asked.

"Sure," the boy replied.

Alien's mustache was itchy, so he ripped it off.

"I'm Alien," he said.

"I'm George," the boy replied, letting the balloon go and kindly tying Alien to the string so he wouldn't float away. "What brings you to Earth?"

Alien explained the situation, feeling sadder by the minute.

George listened carefully. When Alien finished telling him about the problem, George said, "We can fix this! Come on. Let's go to the hardware store."

Alien didn't know what a hardware store was, but he was willing to try anything.

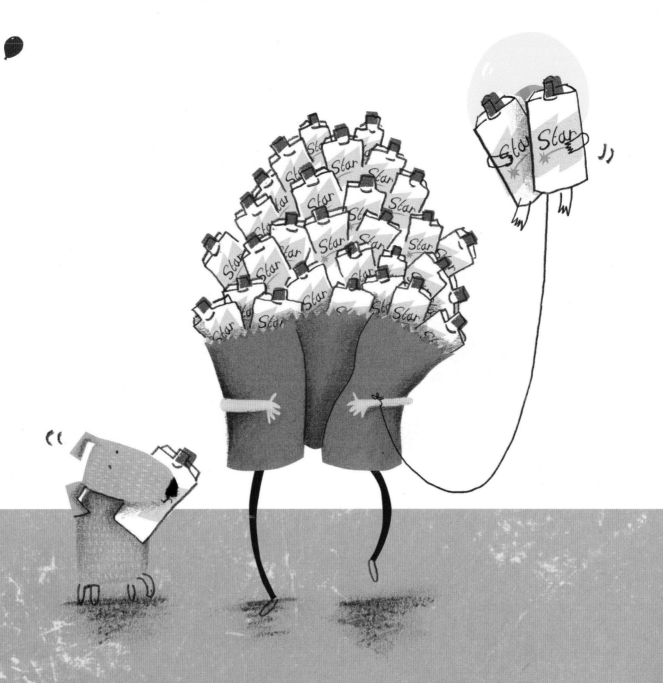

At the hardware store, George knew exactly where to find the magic star varnish. They wasted no time stocking up.

"Do you want to play with me for a while?"
George asked.

Alien wasn't sure. He needed to get the stars
back on, but George had been so helpful.

"Okay," Alien said.

Alien couldn't believe how wonderful it was
to play. He had never had so much fun!

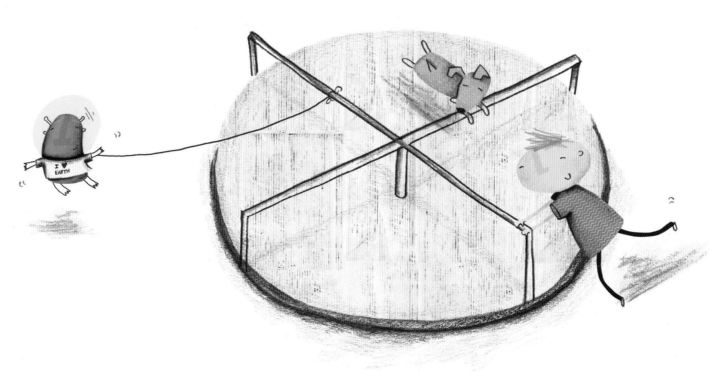

They
giggled
and
giggled
and
giggled.

Alien felt very strange. His body felt light, and he couldn't stop smiling. He was happy!

Then something extraordinary happened . . .

. . . the stars turned on!

"How did you do that?" George asked.

"I didn't," said Alien. "You did! You made me happy! I didn't need magic star varnish after all. I just needed a friend."

"Let's promise to stay friends forever," George said. "That way, the stars will never go out again."

And together, they're still
keeping that promise.